When Michelle wakes up feeling ill on the morning of her seventh birthday, she knows it's not going to be the greatest day of her life. Her mum and dad are still in bed; there's no post because it's a Sunday and then she gets a boring old pair of slippers from her aunt in Canada.

But the slippers are no ordinary pair of slippers – they can talk. They turn out to be the most fantastic present Michelle has ever had and together they have hours of fun. The trouble is that the slippers only talk to sick children and very soon Michelle is better!

Gyles Brandreth was born in 1948 and graduated from Oxford University in 1970 with a degree in Modern Languages. Since then he has had a busy and varied career, and has had more than fifty books published on a whole range of topics. He has also written television scripts and is a well-known broadcaster. Gyles is the founder of the Teddy Bear Museum in Stratford-upon-Avon and the chairman of the National Playing Fields Association, the charity that protects and improves playgrounds and play space throughout the United Kingdom. Gyles became the Member of Parliament for Chester in 1992.

Gyles Brandreth

The Slippers
That Talked

Illustrated by
Annie Horwood

PUFFIN BOOKS

PUFFIN BOOKS

Published by the Penguin Group
Penguin Books Ltd, 27 Wrights Lane, London W8 5TZ, England
Penguin Books USA Inc., 375 Hudson Street, New York, New York 10014, USA
Penguin Books Australia Ltd, Ringwood, Victoria, Australia
Penguin Books Canada Ltd, 10 Alcorn Avenue, Toronto, Ontario, Canada M4V 3B2
Penguin Books (NZ) Ltd, 182–190 Wairau Road, Auckland 10, New Zealand

Penguin Books Ltd, Registered Offices: Harmondsworth, Middlesex, England

First published by Viking 1990
Published in Puffin Books 1992
10 9 8 7 6 5 4 3

Text copyright © Gyles Brandreth, 1990
Illustrations copyright © Annie Horwood, 1990
All rights reserved

The moral right of the author has been asserted

Printed in England by Clays Ltd, St Ives plc
Filmset in Linotron Times

Contents

Chapter One
Happy
Birthday

At long last the great day had arrived.

Michelle had been looking forward to her birthday for months and months. She had been looking forward to it for eleven months and thirty days to be exact. She had always wanted to be seven years old, because seven was her lucky number. Seven, she felt, was a grown-up sort of age and she was, she felt, a grown-up sort of person.

Michelle lived with her mum

and her dad

and a dog called Dog

and a cat called Cat

8

in a house called the Cottage in a tiny village called Snitterfield.

Michelle loved her home and her mum and dad. She loved Dog. She had loved Cat too until the day last summer when Cat got into her bedroom and ate her goldfish (who was called Willie). When Cat ate Willie – which was a natural thing for a cat to do, but horrid all the same – Michelle said to herself, "I will never ever EVER talk to Cat again." And she hadn't.

Michelle talked to Dog a lot. Dog was her best friend really. She told him all her secrets.

And because Dog was a dog, he was very trustworthy and he never told those secrets to anyone.

On the night before her birthday, as she was on her way

up to bed, Michelle said to Dog, "Tomorrow, Dog, is my seventh birthday and it's going to be the best day of my whole life."

It wasn't. It was the worst.

At six o'clock in the morning, Michelle woke up. She expected to feel excited. Instead, she felt sick. She had a sore throat and a thick feeling in her head. She tried to go back to sleep but she couldn't, so she spent an hour lying on her back, gazing at the ceiling and feeling rather uncomfortable, unhappy and odd.

At seven o'clock, she got out of bed and felt a little dizzy. She went across to Mum and Dad's bedroom and found them both asleep. So she went back to her own room, clambered

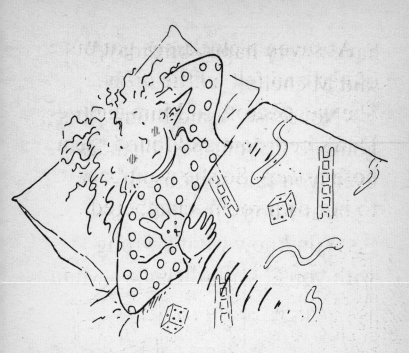

into bed and spent another
hour gazing at the ceiling and
feeling a bit sad and a bit sick.

At eight o'clock, Mum came
into Michelle's room looking
very jolly and singing "Happy
Birthday to You".

"I don't think I'm going to

have a very happy birthday,"
said Michelle.

"Nonsense," said Mum. "It's
going to be your best birthday
ever, you said so yourself."

"But I don't fee–"

"You know what's wrong
with you?" said Michelle's Mum.

"You're hungry. Throw on your clothes and let's get some food inside you. You can open your presents after breakfast."

"Yes, I need breakfast," Michelle said to herself as she got out of bed.

When she was dressed and half-way down the stairs, a happy thought came to Michelle: "Birthday cards! There'll be heaps and heaps of birthday cards!" She rushed to the front door to find them. There was Cat on the mat, but no cards: it was Sunday, so there was no post. Michelle felt

very gloomy. Cat gave her a
friendly "Miaow". Michelle
stomped off to the kitchen.

Michelle's Mum had made a
marvellous breakfast and
Michelle gobbled up the lot –
cereal, scrambled egg, toast
and jam, and hot chocolate.
When she had finished she felt
a little better, but not much.

At nine o'clock, Michelle's Dad marched into the kitchen singing "Happy Birthday to You" and carrying a bundle of presents and cards. Michelle had expected hundreds and

hundreds of presents. In fact,
there were just six and they
looked very small. Three of
them were so small they were
only wrapped in envelopes!

Present Number One was a
book token, and came from
Auntie Lil who lived in
London. Boring!

Present Number Two was

another book token, and came from Auntie Nell who lived in Leeds. Boring!

Present Number Three turned out not to be a present at all, but just a boring birthday card from miserable, mean old Uncle Derek who lived in Dubai. Boring, boring, boring!

Present Number Four was a Yo-Yo from Dog. (It was

actually Michelle's Mum who had bought the Yo-Yo and wrapped it up, but Dog had definitely been with her at the time.)

Present Number Five was from Mum and Dad, and it was a writing-set, complete with two pens, two pencils, a ruler, a rubber and some flowery notepaper with lined envelopes to match. It was a lovely writing-set. Michelle thought it was a very boring birthday present.

Present Number Six was the Big One.

It was a doll, a very special doll that could open and close

its eyes, laugh, cry and even
wee. As Michelle unwrapped
the doll, she thought to herself,
"I'm seven years old, I don't

want a doll – even a doll that can wee. I want a goldfish, a goldfish like Willie."

"Do you like her?" asked Dad.

"Yes, she's lovely," said Michelle, but Dad and Mum knew she didn't really mean it.

At exactly ten o'clock, Michelle was sick.

"Poor Michelle," said Mum. "Let's get you back up to bed."

By eleven o'clock, Michelle was tucked up in bed and fast asleep. She slept non-stop for twenty hours.

Chapter Two
The Surprise
Parcel

When Michelle woke up, she found Mum standing by her bed.

"How do you feel this morning, Michelle?"

"A little better, I think," said Michelle.

"You'd better stay in bed again today and have a nice rest. If you're no better

tomorrow, I'll take you to the doctor."

At that moment the doorbell rang and Dog began to bark. Michelle could hear Dad call "Coming!" as he made his way to the front door, tripping over Cat on the way. She heard him opening the door.

"Oh, a parcel. That looks interesting. Thank you very much."

"A parcel for me? Yippee!" shouted Michelle, sitting up in bed. "Dad, bring it up, bring it up, quick!"

Dad came running up the

stairs and into Michelle's bedroom. He was holding the parcel behind his back.

"Let me see, let me see!" squealed Michelle.

Dad handed her the parcel.

"Oh," said Michelle, "it's rather small." It was rather small. "And it won't be a goldfish." It wasn't a goldfish.

"I wonder who it's from," said Mum.

Michelle looked at the stamps on the parcel. "Canada," she said. "It's from Auntie Ginny!"

Michelle sounded more

27

excited now. She had never met her Canadian auntie, but she usually sent rather special and unusual presents at Christmas and on birthdays. "It'll be something good!"

It wasn't. It was a pair of slippers. It was a boring old pair of ordinary, every-day bedroom slippers. All right, so one was red and one was blue, and each one had a funny face

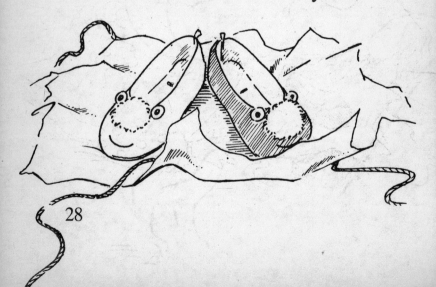

on it, but who wants bedroom
slippers for a seventh birthday
present? Not Michelle, that's
for sure.

"I don't feel very well," said
Michelle, who was suddenly
feeling sick all over again.

"Now don't worry," said

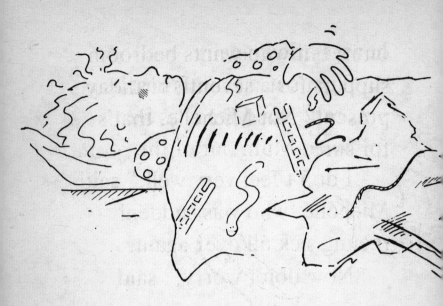

Mum, "you just lie back and rest. Look, I've put a bowl on the floor here if you want to be sick. And if you need me, you just shout. OK?"

"OK," said Michelle, who wasn't feeling at all OK.

"Just get as much rest as you can," said Mum, as she made

her way downstairs.

"That's it, as much rest as
you can," said Dad, as he
followed Mum out of the room.

"Bother!" said Michelle
when her parents had gone.
"Bother!" And she picked
up the slippers and threw them
on to the floor.

31

"Ouch!" said one slipper.

"Ouch!" said the other.

"What do you mean 'ouch'?" said Michelle.

"I mean, that hurt!" said one of the slippers.

"Are you talking to me?" Michelle asked, leaning over the edge of her bed and trying

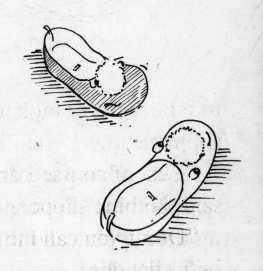

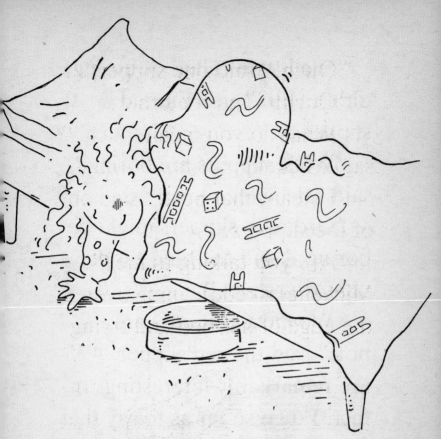

to take a closer look at the
slippers.

"Yes, of course I am, silly,"
said the blue slipper.

"Don't you call me silly,"
said Michelle.

33

"Well, you called us boring, didn't you?" said the red slipper.

"Well, slippers are boring," said Michelle.

"Ordinary slippers might be boring," said the blue slipper, "but we're not."

"We most certainly are not," said the red slipper. "We are remarkably interesting. In fact, I'd go so far as to say that we are the most interesting slippers in the whole wide world."

"I agree!" said Michelle, who could hardly believe her ears. Or her eyes, because now she

had picked up the slippers and
was taking a close look at them.
When the slippers spoke, their
lips moved.

"You really are talking to
me, aren't you?"

"We sure are," said the blue slipper, and he gave Michelle a friendly wink.

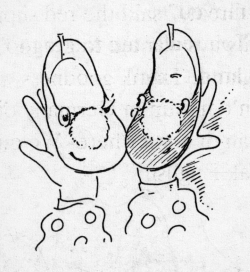

"Where do you come from?" asked Michelle.

"Canada," said the red slipper. "That's why we talk this way. Where do you come from?"

"Snitterfield," said Michelle.

"Where's that?"

"In England."

"Great," said the red slipper. "I always wanted to get to England. Thank goodness we didn't end up in Germany or Japan or somewhere. We only speak English."

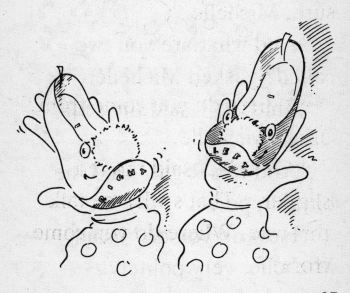

"And a bit of French," added his friend.

"What's your name then, little girl?" asked the red slipper.

"Michelle," said Michelle. "And I'm not a little girl. I'm seven."

"Begging your pardon, I'm sure, Michelle."

"And what are you two called?" asked Michelle.

"I'm Left," said the red slipper.

"And I'm Right,' said the blue slipper.

"How do you do?" said Michelle, very politely.

"You must be sick," said Left.

"Yes, I am," said Michelle, suddenly remembering her sore throat and her headache. "Just a bit. How did you guess?"

"We can only talk to people when they're ill," said Left, with a chuckle.

"When you get better we'll just be ordinary slippers," said Right, "ordinary and boring like all the other slippers in the world."

"But right now," said Left, "we're amazing!"

"You certainly are," said Michelle.

Chapter Three
Fun and Games

"Now we're here, what shall we do?" asked Right, opening his eyes very wide.

"Let's play a game," said Left.

"Let's play 'I Spy'," said Michelle.

So Michelle and Left and Right played "I Spy". And when they'd had enough of

that, Michelle decided to tell
them a story. It was the story
of Cinderella. They had heard
it before, but they were too
polite to say so. Then Left told
Michelle an old Canadian fairy
tale.

Left was just getting to a
scary bit, all about a great big

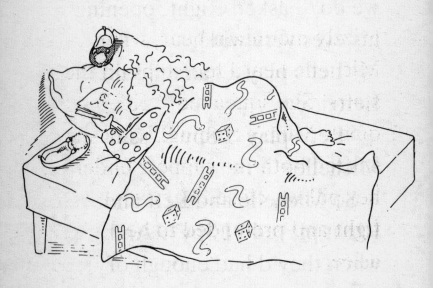

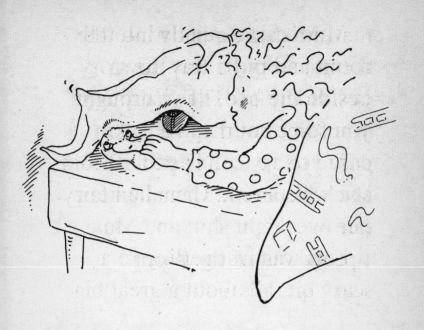

grizzly mountain-bear, when
Michelle heard footsteps on the
stairs. She squeaked: "Keep
quiet, Mum's coming!" and she
stuffed both the slippers under
her pillow, closed her eyes
tight and pretended to be
asleep.

Mum came quietly into the room and put a tray down beside the bed. "I've brought you some soup and a roll in case you're feeling peckish," she whispered. Michelle kept her eyes tight shut and Mum tiptoed out of the room.

From under the pillow,
Michelle heard muffled shouts.
"Help! Help! Let us out! We
can't breathe."

Michelle pulled the slippers
out as fast as she could.

"Sorry," she said.

"That's OK," said the slippers.

"Now where was I?" said Left. "Oh yes. At that moment, the great, grey, grizzly bear was coming out of his cave . . ."

And as Michelle tucked into her soup and roll, Left finished the story. Then it was Right's turn to tell a story. Then it was time to play another game. And another. And another.

Then Michelle heard footsteps on the stairs again.

"Don't put us under the pillow again, *please*," said Left.

"We'll keep quiet, I promise," said Right.

Mum came into the room.
"Well, you look a lot better!
I've brought you some tea.
When you've finished you can
come downstairs and watch
television with us, if you like."

47

"No thanks, Mum," said Michelle. "I think I'll have an early night."

"Good idea," said Mum. "Don't forget to brush your teeth. Good-night. I'll check you later."

48

"Don't bother, Mum, I'll be all right. Good-night."

When Mum had gone, Michelle offered the slippers one of her sandwiches.

"No thanks," said Left, "we're not hungry."

"We never are. We don't need to eat and we don't need to drink and we don't even need to sleep," said Right. "But you do, Michelle, so we mustn't stay up all night chattering."

When Michelle had finished her tea, she got out of bed to put the tray on the landing so her mother wouldn't need to come into her room again that night.

"Put us on," said Left.

"Yes," said Right. "Try us out for size."

"Are you sure it won't hurt? I'm quite heavy, you know."

"Nonsense," said Right, "we're slippers. We're made for wearing. If you don't put us on, we won't get any exercise."

Michelle slipped her feet into the slippers. They felt warm and cosy.

"It's a great fit, isn't it?" said Left.

"Sure is," said Right.

Michelle wore the slippers to the bathroom, where she cleaned her teeth and went to the lavatory. In case you're wondering, the slippers closed

their eyes while Michelle went to the lavatory. They were *very* polite.

When Michelle woke up the next day, she still had a sore throat. She still had a pair of talking slippers too.

"Good morning, Left," Michelle said to the red slipper.

"Good morning, Right," Michelle said to the blue slipper.

"Good morning, Michelle," said the slippers brightly. "How are you feeling today?"

"I've still got a sore throat but I'm feeling much better, thank you."

"What are we going to do today?" asked the slippers.

"Let's take Dog for a walk," suggested Michelle.

"What's Dog?" asked Right, looking puzzled.

"Dog's a dog," said
Michelle, laughing. "Don't you
have dogs in Canada?"

"We have hot dogs," said
Left. "They're sausages that
come in buns. I've never tried
one, but I believe they're
delicious."

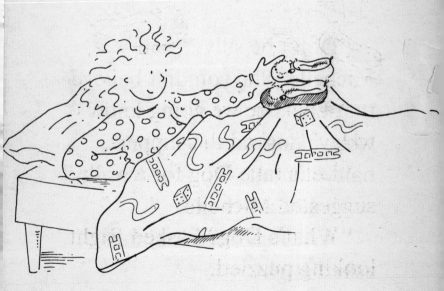

"Don't be silly," said
Michelle. She couldn't believe
that the slippers didn't know
what a dog was. "A dog's a
hairy animal with four legs and
a tail and a wet nose."

"Are dogs fierce animals?"
asked Right.

56

"They can be," said Michelle, "but they're friendly too."

"I'd like to meet a dog," said Left.

"Me too," said Right.

"You can – right now," said Michelle.

"Right now?" asked Right,

sounding very surprised. "Are we going to the zoo?"

"No," laughed Michelle, "I'm going to fetch Dog."

Michelle jumped out of bed and ran on to the landing.

"Dog," she called. "Here, boy!"

Dog was in the kitchen finishing his breakfast, but as soon as he heard Michelle's voice he came bounding up the stairs, wagging his tail.

"Come and meet my friends," said Michelle, leading Dog into the bedroom.

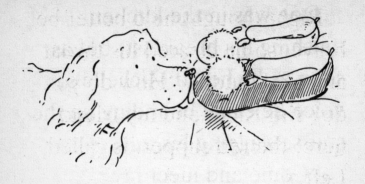

Left and Right were perched on the end of Michelle's bed. They were quite small slippers and Dog was quite a large dog. As he came up to them, they felt a little frightened.

Dog sniffed at the slippers.

"What's he doing?" whispered Left.

"He's getting to know you," said Michelle. "That's the way dogs do it."

Right thought he'd better be brave, so he cleared his throat and said loudly, "How do you do? I'm Right and my friend here, the red slipper, is called Left."

"Pleased to meet you, I'm sure," said Left, rather nervously.

The slippers had never seen a sniffing dog before. Dog had never seen talking slippers before either, so when he heard the slippers make a noise he didn't like it.

Dog growled.

"Help!" yelped Left. "He's going to eat us!"

"Don't be silly," said Michelle. "He's just not used to you, that's all."

"Now be a good boy," Michelle said to Dog, patting him. "They're my birthday present from Auntie Ginny in Canada. And they're special slippers, because when you're ill they can talk to you. They like you, Dog."

Michelle gave Dog another pat. She said to the slippers, "You like Dog, don't you?"

"Er – yes, of course," said Left and Right rather timidly,

as they tried to show Dog their friendliest smiles.

Dog must have liked their smiles, because he stopped growling and started sniffing again. Then he put out his tongue and began licking the slippers.

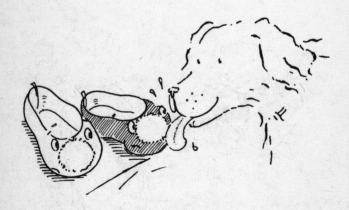

"Ooh, that tickles," said Left.

"What's he doing?" squealed

Right, as Dog's big wet tongue slurped around his ears.

"He's showing you he likes you," said Michelle.

Having given the slippers a good lick, Dog decided to pick them up, and he picked them up the way dogs do – in his mouth.

"Help! Help!" shouted Right.

"He is going to eat us after all!" cried Left.

"No, he's not," said Michelle, "he's wagging his tail."

"What does that mean?" asked Left.

"He's happy," said Michelle.

"Of course he's happy," muttered Right. "He's going to have slippers for breakfast."

Suddenly the slippers and Michelle and Dog realized that Dad was standing in the doorway.

"Did I hear someone say kippers for breakfast?" he asked.

"No," said Michelle. "I
mean – yes," she added. "I'd
love kippers for breakfast."

"What's Dog doing with your
new slippers?" asked Dad. "He
looks as if he wants to take
them for a walk."

Dog wagged his tail.

"I'd like to go for a walk

today," said Michelle.

"You must be feeling better," said Dad.

When Dad had gone downstairs for breakfast, Dog let go of the slippers. He didn't drop them. He put them gently back on the end of Michelle's bed.

"Are you two all right?" asked Michelle.

"Yes, thank you," said Right.

"Shall we all go for a walk after breakfast?" said Michelle. "It could be quite an adventure."

Chapter Four
Making a
Splash

It was quite an adventure!

Mum said that Michelle
wasn't well enough yet for a
long walk, but that she and Dog
and Dad could go out for five
minutes – to the pond and back.

After breakfast, when she
had cleaned her teeth and
tidied her hair, Michelle and
Dad and Dog and the slippers

set off for their walk. Dog
carried the slippers in his
mouth. It wasn't the most
comfortable way for Left and
Right to travel, but it was exciting.

Because Dad was with them,

the slippers didn't talk. But they kept their eyes open and looked all around them, as Dog trotted down the village lane to the pond.

When they got there, they saw Tiggy Smith sitting on the bench by the water. Michelle didn't like Tiggy Smith. He was a boy with red hair and freckles, who was in the same class as Michelle at school. Michelle didn't like Tiggy because he had once pulled her hair.

Dad didn't know this so he said, "Hello, Tiggy, what are you doing here?"

"Nothing much," said Tiggy, throwing a pebble into the pond. "In fact, I'm going home now. Goodbye."

As he turned to go, Tiggy picked up a large piece of wood that was lying on the ground and, as he wandered off towards his house, he threw the stick into the water.

Now, if you know anything about dogs and sticks and water, you will know what happened next. One of the things that dogs love most in all the world is having a stick thrown into a pond for them to go and fetch.

The moment Dog saw Tiggy throw that stick into the water, he was off. Of course, he quite forgot that he had a pair of talking slippers in his mouth. He bounded straight into the water – SPLASH! – and

started swimming towards the stick.

"Help! Help!" yelped Left.

"What are you doing, Dog?" cried Right. "We can't swim. Help! Help!"

But Dog wasn't listening. He was too excited. He was swimming towards Tiggy's stick as fast as his paws would carry him. When he reached the stick, he let go of the slippers

and took hold of the piece of
wood instead.

"Help! Help!" shouted the
slippers. "We're going to sink!"

But they didn't sink. They
floated. As Dog swam back
with his piece of wood, Left
and Right bobbed about in the
middle of the pond. The sun

was shining and the water was
warm, and once they'd got over
the shock of it all, the slippers
decided that they were quite
enjoying their surprise dip.

79

Michelle wasn't enjoying it at all. Dog had returned with Tiggy's stick instead of her slippers. Dog was very pleased with himself.

"Naughty Dog," said Michelle. "Go fetch the slippers."

But Dog was too busy shaking himself and splashing water everywhere to hear what Michelle was saying.

"Oh, Dad," pleaded Michelle, "we've got to rescue the slippers or they'll drown."

"Slippers can't drown," said Dad. "They'll just sink."

"These ones can drown, Dad. Oh, do something, Dad, please."

Michelle sounded so
desperate that Dad did do
something. He took off his

shoes and his socks (there was a
hole in the left one) and rolled
up his trouser legs. Then he
waded out into the pond. It
wasn't very deep, but it was
very wet and it seemed a long
way to the middle.

Michelle shouted

encouragingly from the edge:
"Keep going, Dad, you're a
hero!"

Dad did keep going and he
was a hero. He reached the
slippers and he lifted them
safely out of the water.

"Thank you," said Left.

"Yes, thank you, thank you, thank you," said Right.

As soon as they got home Dad had a hot bath, Mum dried Dog with an old towel, and Michelle put the slippers into the toasty-warm airing-cupboard to dry.

By tea-time, Left and Right had dried out completely and were back where they belonged – on Michelle's feet.

"I still don't see how it happened," said Mum.

"It was Tiggy Smith's fault," said Michelle. "He threw a stick into the pond and Dog went for it."

Dog looked up from his basket and gently wagged his tail.

"You know," said Dad, scratching his head, "when I

picked up those slippers, I'm sure I heard them say 'thank you'."

"Don't be silly," said Mum, "slippers can't talk."

"Tishoo!" Somebody sneezed.

"Bless you!" said Mum.

"It wasn't me," said Michelle.

"It wasn't me," said Dad.

"Tishoo!" Somebody sneezed again. And this time Michelle and Mum and Dad realized that the sneeze was coming from under the table.

"Tishoo! Tishoo!"

Left was having a sneezing fit.

Mum and Dad and Michelle
looked under the table and
there, by Michelle's feet, sat
Cat.

"It was only Cat," said Mum.

"Was it?" asked Dad.

"Of course it was," said Michelle. And she thought to herself, "Cat's not such a bad cat after all."

Chapter Five
Getting Better

Michelle and Left and Right went up to bed after tea. They had had a long and tiring day.

"It was exciting too," said Left, once they were all alone in Michelle's room.

"I like splashing about in ponds," said Right.

"We can do it again tomorrow, if you like," said Michelle.

"Not if you're better," said Right. "We only come out to play when you're under the weather, remember?"

"Still," said Left, "it'll be something to look forward to if ever you are ill again. Have you had chicken-pox?"

"No," said Michelle.

"You're bound to have chicken-pox," said Left. "We can have some fun then."

"What are we going to do tonight?" asked Michelle.

"You need some sleep," said Left.

"Let's tell some stories first," said Michelle. "I'd like to stay up all night telling stories."

Left and Right and Michelle didn't stay up all night telling stories, but they did stay up very, very late. They were still chattering away when Mum and Dad came up to bed and tiptoed into Michelle's room to see if she was all right.

Michelle had turned off her light so Mum couldn't see that she was lying on her back, holding the slippers in front of her face.

It was eleven o'clock before Michelle fell asleep. Left was in

the middle of a story about a
gentle giant who wanted to be a
ballet dancer, but couldn't find
a ballet school to take him,
when Michelle finally dozed
off. She fell asleep with a happy
smile on her face.

In the morning she woke up with the same happy smile on her face and the same pair of slippers on her hands.

"Good morning, Left," she said to the red slipper.

"Good morning, Right," she said to the blue slipper.

There was no reply.

"I say, wake up you two. I said 'Good Morning'."

Michelle shook the slippers. The slippers didn't say a word. Quickly, Michelle climbed out of bed and put them on. "This'll wake them up," she thought, and she danced and danced around the room.

94

"How's that for a bit of
exercise, eh?" she said,
kneeling down to take a closer

look at their faces. Their eyes
were closed and their mouths
were shut. Then Michelle
realized what had happened.
She was better.

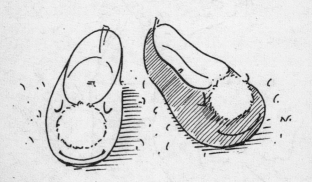